Five Birdies

Rosie Bumgardner

Illustrated by Warner McGee

LifeRich Publishing is a registered trademark of The Reader's Digest Association, Inc.

LifeRich Publishing books may be ordered through booksellers or by contacting:

LifeRich Publishing
1663 Liberty Drive
Bloomington, IN 47403
www.liferichpublishing.com
844-686-9607

ISBN: 978-1-4897-3599-7 (sc)
ISBN: 978-1-4897-3600-0 (hc)
ISBN: 978-1-4897-3601-7 (e)

Print information available on the last page.

LifeRich Publishing rev. date: 08/04/2021

Written by Rosie Bumgardner

Illustrated by Warner McGee

This book is dedicated to my
beautiful daughter, Jenny,
who is my inspiration.

Once upon a time, there were five birdies: a red birdie, an orange birdie, a yellow birdie, a green birdie, and a blue birdie.

One sunny day, the five birdies decided to go to the park.

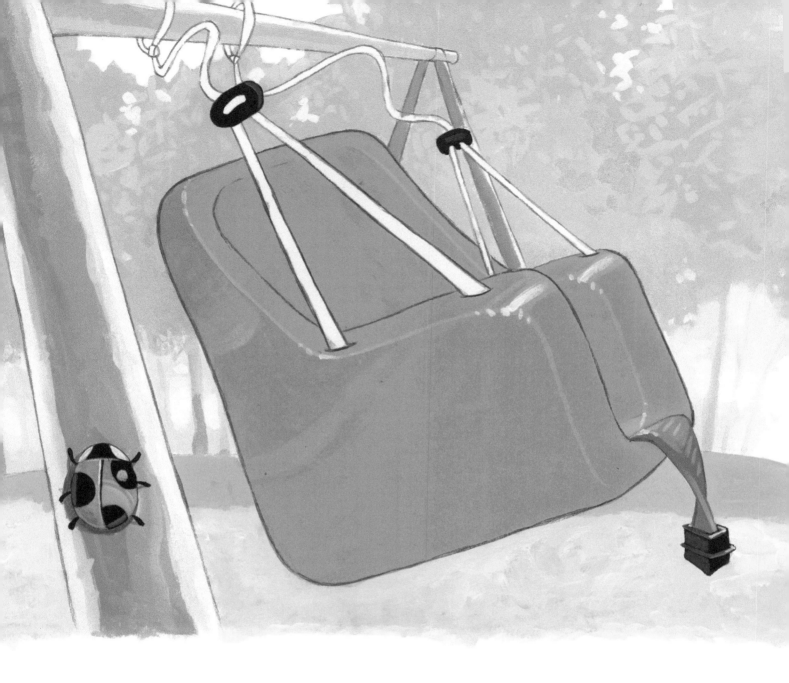

The first birdie to arrive at the park was Carl, the red cardinal. When Carl got to the park, he saw a red swing.

"Hey, that swing is red just like me,"
said Carl. "Do you see something else
that is red just like me?"

The second birdie to arrive at the park was Oscar, the orange oriole. When Oscar got to the park, he saw an orange slide.

"Hey, that slide is orange just like me," said Oscar. "Do you see something else that is orange just like me?"

The third birdie to arrive at the park was Connie, the yellow canary. When Connie got to the park, she saw a yellow tunnel.

"Hey, that tunnel is yellow just like me,"
said Connie. "Do you see something else
that is yellow just like me?"

The fourth birdie to arrive at the park was Patsy, the green parrot. When Patsy got to the park, she saw a green merry-go-round.

"Hey, that merry-go-round is green just like me," said Patsy. "Do you see something else that is green just like me?"

The fifth birdie to arrive at the park was Buster, the blue jay. When Buster got to the park, he saw a blue seesaw.

"Hey, that seesaw is blue just like me," said Buster. "Do you see something else that is blue just like me?"

The five birdies played at the park
all afternoon. When it was time
to go home, they lifted their
wings and flew towards the sky.

Suddenly, they noticed a beautiful rainbow that was green, blue, red, orange, and yellow just like them.

The End

Lightning Source UK Ltd.
Milton Keynes UK
UKHW052226160821
388952UK00006B/371